ZORA
AND THE
GREYHOUNDS

ZORA AND THE GREYHOUNDS

Mark AJ Guilliatt

BEMIS PARK
PUBLISHING

Omaha, Nebraska

A special thanks again to my Mom and Dad and Theresa for being so supportive of this project. It took a little longer than I thought to turn an inkling of an idea into a reality—a reality that I couldn't have brought to fruition without the logistical, layout, editing, and all around support and patience of Lisa Pelto and her staff: Ellie, Rachel, and Sarah.

BlueBerry Illustrations, thanks so much for providing the artwork that captured the soul of Zora's story.

Thanks to Dossett, Mila, and Wiley for being such a fabulous captive audience.

Also, thanks to Lylie and Mia for giving Zora's story one of its first reads.

And thanks to everyone else for their input, support, and/or inspiration—especially, Myrtle, Priscilla, Nyakim, Joyce, Mrs. Bridges, Hanscom Park Dog Park, and Bemis Park Publishing.

ISBN13: 978-0-9975002-1-9
Library of Congress Cataloging Number: 2016938622

Published by Bemis Park Publishing
c/o Concierge Marketing, 13518 L. Street, Omaha, NE, 68137
BemisPark@conciergemarketing.com

www.BemisParkPublishing.com
www.ZorasAdventures.com

Illustrated by: BlueBerry.com
Design, production and marketing: Concierge Marketing Inc.

Printed in the United States of America
10 9 8 7 6 5 4 3 2

Based on true events.

ZORA AND THE GREYHOUNDS

Chapter 1

Not that long ago near a park not that far away lived two puppies named Zora and Jackie.

Zora was adorable with her black curly coat, and she was extraordinarily speedy. People couldn't believe it when they saw such a small dog run so incredibly fast. They would ask Mark what kind of dog Zora was. Mark liked to tell these folks, with a little sparkle in his eye, that Zora was a first generation American Squirrel Hound.

Now, you and I know that Zora wasn't really an American Squirrel Hound, since no such breed exists. But she was really a mixed breed—part Poodle, part Cocker Spaniel, sprinkled with a little bit of Pekingese. A beautiful mix, but she was not a purebred.

Most folks knew Mark was just kidding around, but Zora often overheard Mark call her an American Squirrel Hound. So, by and by, she began to believe that she was a one-of-a-kind breed—an American Squirrel Hound.

Jackie, on the other hand, was a purebred Yorkshire Terrier with a dignified family history and she was proud of that fact. Besides her bold personality, the only thing big about this cute little Yorkie was her big ears. Zora and Jackie's backgrounds were quite different, but they had become the best of friends while living together with Mark.

One of the things that Zora and Jackie loved most was going to the park where they could run and play with all the other types of dogs. There were big dogs and little dogs. Thick dogs and thin dogs. Some were fast and some were furry. Most of the dogs liked to race and wrestle. Sometimes Jackie preferred to be a lap dog. So she would jump up on Mark's lap while all the other dogs raced around chasing balls and tails around the park.

One day Speedy, the Greyhound, was at the park. Zora and Speedy began to race around the park. The other dogs gasped, "Jeez!" as Zora kept up with Speedy paw for paw.

"Never seen that before," said Larry, a big Black Lab.

"Me neither," chimed in Harry, the Husky.

"Yeah. Wow! No one has ever kept up with Speedy before," agreed a pretty pink Poodle named Avery.

Even Speedy was surprised to see Zora keep up stride for stride. "Holy Toledo! You can really zoom, Zora," panted Speedy as he caught his breath.

"Gosh, thanks Speedy. I love to run. You are very fast, too," replied Zora.

"Of course I am, Zora. I am a Greyhound. I am a retired racing dog." Speedy touted, kind of matter-of-factly.

"A racing dog? Cool. How can I become a racing dog?" asked Zora.

Speedy chuckled. "Zora, you aren't a Greyhound. You're a mutt. Mutts can't race at the dog tracks."

Zora looked surprised and said, "What do you mean I'm a mutt? I'm an American Squirrel Hound."

Speedy's chuckle turned into a laugh, and all the other dogs began to laugh too. "There is no such breed. You are mixed up. You are a mixed breed—a mutt! And mutts can't run at the dog track." Speedy concluded. Now all the other dogs were really laughing.

Jackie heard all the commotion, jumped off of Mark's lap and sprinted over to see what was happening. She ran to Zora's side and said, "Zora, let's go home." She knew that Zora's feelings were hurt. Zora was trying hard to hold back her tears. Just a moment ago, when she was running with Speedy, she was so very happy. Now she just wanted to run away. Zora put her tail between her legs and slinked away with her best friend Jackie.

ZORA AND THE GREYHOUNDS

Chapter 2

Jackie and Zora jumped into the car. Mark started the engine and back home they went. Jackie, as usual, had pointed her little face out the window. But Zora just curled up on the back seat. She didn't feel like herself.

As they pulled up to the house, Jackie jumped out of the car. "Come on Zora. We are home now. You don't have to worry about all those other dogs. You were faster than Speedy by at least a nose. Come on. Let's get our treat," Jackie barked.

Zora didn't budge. She stayed curled up in the backseat. Mark saw that something was wrong with Zora. "Zora, let's go inside," he said. She still wasn't in the mood to move. Mark noticed that Zora looked very sad, so he picked her up in his arms and carried her inside.

Zora sat quietly by the French doors for a long time. She stared out the window noticing the squirrels scampering around the yard, but they just didn't excite her today. As usual, Jackie started barking at the squirrels, but Zora just buried her head in her paws.

"I am not a special breed. I am not an American Squirrel Hound. I am really just a mutt. And I can't race with the Greyhounds," she thought.

Jackie saw that Zora wasn't her old self. Without saying a word, Jackie laid down next to her. Zora still wasn't in the mood to talk, but she loved having her best friend by her side. Zora knew that Jackie understood. The next day after they got back from their walk around the block Jackie said, "Zora, you still seem a little sad. I hope you aren't letting those other dogs get to you."

After a moment, Zora responded, "I know I shouldn't, but they really hurt my feelings. And what they said is true. So maybe I shouldn't go back to the park. I'm just a mutt. I'm not a purebred like you."

"I don't care what the other dogs say. You've been my best friend since you first came to live with us in the big white house. Maybe you aren't a purebred, but you are even better than that, Zora. You are an original dog. No other dog is just like you," Jackie cheerfully yipped.

Zora wasn't convinced. Her heart was still stinging from what Speedy had said to her the day before. "I wish that made a difference. Even if I am an original dog, they won't let me race at the dog tracks," muttered Zora.

"Didn't you edge out Speedy when you were both racing around the park?" asked Jackie.

"Yes, I did. Didn't I?" Zora timidly answered.

"Do you think you could beat Speedy in another race?" Jackie asked.

"Well. I suppose if I set my mind to it and I trained properly," Zora responded.

"Wherever we go, Zora, people always tell Mark how fast you are. They always say that they have never seen a dog run as fast as you before," Jackie reminded Zora.

"I guess I am pretty fast," Zora acknowledged. Zora was starting to feel better. She felt very lucky to have such a loyal and loving friend like Jackie.

"Zora, I know you're fast. You are always leaving me in the dust. You always get to the dog food before I do and you always get to the fire hydrant first," Jackie added.

Zora started to smile. Zora started to believe in herself again. She wasn't sure how she would get to race the other dogs, but she knew she was one of the fastest dogs around.

But Jackie wasn't just trying to make Zora feel better. She really believed that Zora could race with the big dogs of dog racing. "Zora, we need to get you a tryout for the dog races!" exclaimed Jackie.

"How are we going to do that?" asked Zora.

"First we have to get you prepared. It's not going to be easy. You really have to go for it. Can you do what it takes today, tomorrow, the next day, and all the days after that until you get your chance?"

Zora didn't hesitate. She barked as loud as she could, "Let's go for it!"

The next day Zora skipped the ice cream treat Mark had set down for her. She instead found the leftover broccoli and kale that Mark had put in her bowl. She knew she better eat only healthy food if she really wanted to get a shot at racing the greyhounds. Jackie and Zora gobbled up her healthy breakfast, then she and Jackie headed out to the yard. Their normal routine was to run over to the edge of their yard to bark at the squirrels on the other side of the fence, but today they decided to just run laps around the house. It was a hot summer day. Even though they were really panting, they kept going. To keep Zora motivated Jackie was training right along with Zora—nipping at her tail.

Mark stepped onto the porch and saw his dogs zipping around the house. "What's gotten into you two? You're so fast you're making me dizzy!" Mark marveled. It was very hot, but neither dog was slowing down. Zora and Jackie were thirsty.

"Zora, Mark just brought our water bowls outside. We better get a drink. We don't want to overheat," Jackie said, panting.

"Not yet. I want to keep going!" barked Zora.

"Zora, this is only the first day of training. All this hard work and heat might make you a sick puppy. We will be back at it tomorrow, and the next day, and the next day after that," reminded Jackie.

"I'm just so excited. I never want to quit. But I guess it's okay to rest up so we can work out again tomorrow." Zora replied as she came to a screeching halt in front of the water bowl. Jackie wasn't prepared for Zora's sudden pit stop, got tripped up and landed right in the water bowl! Both dogs couldn't stop laughing as Jackie shook herself dry.

ZORA AND THE GREYHOUNDS

Chapter 3

Throughout the summer, even through crashing thunder, lightning, and rain, Zora and Jackie kept up their relentless backyard routine. Nothing seemed to slow them down.

Mark had spent all summer watching them race around the house. "I don't know what's gotten into you two, but ever since our last trip to the park you've really been committed to your training. Jackie you are one heck of a motivator because Zora is faster than ever! Maybe it's about time we go back to the dog park." Mark called for Zora and Jackie to join him in the car.

"Zora, Mark wants to take us back to the park. Are you ready to go back?" asked Jackie.

Zora hesitated for a moment. She hadn't forgotten how all the dogs had laughed at her and hurt her feelings the last time they were there. She wasn't sure if she was ready.

"We've worked hard this summer. I know you are ready. I believe in you, Zora! Believe in yourself!" demanded little Jackie.

Jackie asked again, "Are you ready to go back, Zora?"

"Yes, that's what I am going to do. I want to race Speedy again. I hope he's at the park today. Let's go!" Zora barked.

Zora and Jackie raced up to the car and jumped right in. They both poked their heads out the window as Mark headed down the alley. Their tails were wagging wildly as the car zipped through town to the park.

And as luck would have it, they saw Speedy just as they pulled up to the park. Speedy was pulling away from a pack of dogs as they all chased after a ball. Zora gulped. "He really is fast. What if I can't beat Speedy this time?" she wondered. Then she remembered how much Jackie believed in her. She knew she had to try. She took a deep breath. When Mark opened the door, Zora and Jackie sprang from the car and sprinted to the park.

"Hey! Look who's here," howled Larry the Black Lab.

"What do you know? It looks like Lady and the Day Dreamer." cracked Harry the Husky.

"Where have you been? Licking your wounds?" chimed in the pretty pink Poodle, Avery.

Some of the other dogs began to laugh. Speedy heard the ruckus. He galloped back over to the pack of dogs that were beginning to surround Zora and Jackie.

Jackie glanced at Zora, giving Zora courage and confidence. This time, Zora wouldn't back down. She took another deep breath. She was nervous. She felt a few tears building up, but she was determined to hold the tears back.

Of course Speedy remembered Zora—and how fast she was. And even though Speedy would never have told anyone, deep down he admired Zora for coming back for a rematch. Just the same, he strolled up to Zora and Jackie. He spoke softly to Jackie, "Hey little lady, why don't you and your pal go home?" The other dogs couldn't quite make out what Speedy was saying.

Jackie's fur bristled and her big ears stood upright, she looked at Zora and said, "I don't like Speedy's tone." Then little Jackie turned to Speedy and barked, "What did you say?"

Seeing Jackie stand up to Speedy gave Zora a feeling of confidence. "If you have something to say to me, go right ahead and say it to me," Zora barked boldly.

The other dogs cocked their ears waiting to hear Speedy's response.

Speedy was a bit surprised that these small dogs were defying his suggestion to go home. So now, with all the other dogs listening he didn't feel like he had much room to backpedal. "I said 'Scram!' Why don't you take your big dreams and your little lady friend and scram! Go back to the funny farm and chase your crazy ideas. Must I remind you that mutts can't race at the dog tracks? You'd be eating my dust anyway," bellowed Speedy.

Jackie growled.

Zora took in a deep breath. She looked Speedy in the eyes. "You can't beat me if I don't quit trying," Zora replied, trying to stay calm.

Just then a tennis ball soared over the dogs into the open field. The bright yellow ball caught their attention as it flew overhead. At that moment, the pack knew the race was on. A young Whippet named Wiley was first out of the blocks. Speedy was a close second as he tore out after the ball. Several other dogs followed in pursuit.

"Zora, GO! Here's your chance! I know you can do it!" hollered Jackie.

Zora sprang into action. She was already several dogs behind the lead dogs. "Catch 'em, Zora! Catch 'em!" Jackie encouraged.

Zora focused on the tennis ball as it continued to roll way out in front of them. She was behind, but she wasn't going to quit. The Whippet hadn't paced himself. He had started out too fast. Zora closed in on him as he faded. Speedy had captured the lead.

Could Zora catch Speedy?

There were still several dogs between them. Zora was gaining ground on Speedy, but the tennis ball was getting closer and closer. The two remaining dogs between Zora and Speedy collided and fell down in a flurry of paws and ears, dirt and grass. Zora ran right between the two tumbling hounds.

She was closing in on Speedy as the tennis ball came to a stop. Speedy and Zora were only a few yards away from the glory of grabbing that bright yellow ball and proving that she was the fastest in the pack. Zora knew all the training was going to pay off. She felt a rush of energy and burst ahead. She reached down and grabbed the tennis ball in her mouth. She did it! She beat Speedy!

A few seconds later Speedy was next to her. Speedy couldn't believe it. He couldn't think of any good excuses. Speedy didn't want to lose, but he prided himself on good sportsmanship. "Zora, you beat me fair and square. You and Jackie deserve to be at the park just like the rest of the dogs. You're part of the canine pack," reckoned Speedy.

"Thanks Speedy," Zora replied. "Jackie wouldn't let me quit."

Speedy said, "I am glad you didn't give up. I really miss the competition of the dog track. I didn't want to retire, but they made me retire. They said I had reached mandatory retirement. Even though I was one of the fastest dogs on the track, they said I was too old for racing. Speedy looked sad.

They built me a new dog house, gave me a lifetime supply of bones, and gave me this gold collar. But I didn't want to stop racing. I should have been more like you, Zora. You didn't quit even when we were all laughing at you. I am sorry I laughed at you, Zora." Speedy smiled and said, "I still don't know how a mutt . . . Ah . . . I mean an American Squirrel Hound like you can race at the dog track. But if they do let a dog other than a Greyhound race, my money is on you."

ZORA AND THE GREYHOUNDS

Chapter 4

*Z*ora was happy that she had proven herself, but her dreams were bigger than one race in the park. She still wanted to figure out how she could race at the dog track. She certainly wasn't going to just rest on her haunches.

While the dogs had been racing down in the park, Tazi, one of the world's most famous racing dogs, stood on a hill above them watching the day's events unfold. He had just noticed a small black mutt and his childhood hero, Speedy, racing. His jaw dropped, and he started pulling hard on his leash toward the dogs to get a closer look. Plus, he wanted his handler to see what he was seeing. "Stay. Stay. Tazi, what's wrong with you boy? Quit tugging on your leash. What's wrong?" asked his handler, Donald P. Prince. Tazi kept barking and pulling, and lunging forward. Mr. Prince saw what had captured Tazi's attention. "Holy flying bats out of the belfry! I see what you are seeing, Tazi. That dog is really moving," exclaimed Mr. Prince.

Tazi barked in agreement. He just witnessed a real underdog-come-from-behind victory. Mr. Prince escorted Tazi down the hill. The other dogs stood in awe as Tazi came into view. They had much admiration for this world champion racer.

"Whose speedy little canine is this?" asked Mr. Prince.

"She lives with me," responded Mark.

"Well. You have quite a little dog there, Mister. Have you given any thought to getting her into racing?" added Mr. Prince.

"I sure like watching her run, but I don't know the first thing about dog racing," admitted Mark.

"Well, it's your lucky day, Mister. You may know my famous dog, Tazi. What you don't know is that without me, Tazi would have just been a regular hound. See, my name is Donald P. Prince. My middle initial is P—P for Promoter. I am Tazi's agent and owner. I make sure that old boy Tazi is a headliner wherever we go. And that has made all the difference between chopped liver and steak for dinner. You see, a good race dog can win some big bucks. I'm not in this just to pick up dog deposits. I am here to make bank deposits. So whaddya say? Need some extra money for your piggy bank?"

"The extra money would sure be nice, but I think it takes quite a bit of money to get a dog registered for the dog races. Isn't that so?" questioned Mark.

"It takes money to make money. And I got the money to make you money. All of Tazi's winnings have made me a rich man. Furthermore—though your little dog is fast—she is still just a mixed breed. She won't be able to race without my connections to the dog racing biz," boasted Mr. Prince. "Without me, son, it can't be done."

" Zora is sure fast. And I know how much she would love to race," Mark pondered out loud.

"Well, son, I can make it happen. If you hand her over and let me promote her, I will pay for all of the registration fees, I will cut you in on a portion of the winnings, and, of course, you would need to grant me custody of Zora while I train her with Tazi for the upcoming race," added Mr. Prince.

Mark knew Zora wouldn't be happy at a training camp with Mr. Prince. And Jackie would be lonely without Zora around the house to play with her. "Mr. Prince, I appreciate the opportunity, but I don't think we can take you up on your offer," replied Mark.

"Suit yourself, son. Racing's my game, and there's nobody better than me. So when you change your mind, don't forget my name," answered Mr. Prince.

Zora was listening to the two men talk. She wanted more than anything to race at the dog tracks, but she didn't want to go away with Mr. Prince. She didn't want to be away from Mark and Jackie. Maybe her dream of becoming a race dog wasn't going to come true after all. She was going to have to just go back to being another ordinary dog.

She had felt like this before when she lived at the dog orphanage. So many people had come to see her, but every day at the end of the day she had to stay in the kennel by herself. She was always so excited to see the people. She always tried to let them know. She jumped the highest and barked the loudest. It was very lonely there. She didn't feel very special when she lived at the orphanage. Now, hearing Mark talk to Mr. Prince, she wondered if Mark and Jackie would ever make her go back to the dog orphanage.

ZORA AND THE GREYHOUNDS

Chapter 5

By now Zora should have known that Mark and Jackie considered her part of the family. They would never send her back to the dog orphanage. But, at this very moment, Zora doubted herself. She didn't know how to make her dream of racing come true. She didn't want to give up on her dream, but how could she let Mark know that she didn't want to give up?

After leaving the park, as usual, Jackie and Zora jumped in Mark's car. Jackie once again poked her head out the window as they zoomed back home. "The fresh air will do you some good," barked Jackie.

Zora jumped from the back seat. She thought Jackie just might be right. She took a deep breath and let the wind blow through her fur. She looked down at Jackie and started wagging her tail. "Jackie, I have an idea. I have an idea!" she barked excitedly.

Mark pulled into the driveway and parked the car. He opened the door to let the dogs out. Zora immediately jumped out the door and ran as fast as she could to the sidewalk. She knew the newspaper would be there. Zora didn't want Mark to forget how fast she was. Plus, she wanted to show Mark that she was willing to work hard in any kind of weather—even if it just meant fetching the paper.

"You are so fast, Zora!" Mark exclaimed. "We aren't going to give up. We are going to get you into the races. How about this idea? Let's get a paper route so we can save up the money we need to get you registered and trained. You can help me deliver the papers and we'll do our route faster than anyone!"

Zora wagged her tail so hard she almost took off in the air. That was just what she wanted! She knew she would have to get up early in the morning to help Mark deliver the papers. But she also knew it would make her faster and stronger, so she could compete with the Greyhounds.

ZORA AND THE GREYHOUNDS

Chapter 6

Nothing stopped Mark and Zora from delivering the papers. After several months of delivering the papers through rain and sleet and even snow and heat, they had saved enough money. But more importantly, Zora was stronger, faster, and more confident that she could do anything.

Mark filled out the entry form and sent it off with the entry fee to the Dog Racing Commission. Every day Mark, Jackie, and Zora would run out to check the mail. A week went by.

Nothing.

Was Zora going to get a chance to race with the big dogs?

"Hi Mark. How are your puppies today?" asked the Postman. "I have a big envelope from the Dog Racing Commission for you."

"You just made our day. Girls, come here," Mark called. "Let's open the envelope together."

"I'm so excited!" barked Jackie.

"I'm nervous. What if they won't let me enter the race?" asked Zora.

"Don't be silly. You are the fastest dog around," reminded Jackie.

Mark opened the envelope. "Give me a high five, Zora! You made it! The race is next Saturday. They want us at the track an hour before the race for check-in."

Zora and Jackie were both so happy.

Next Saturday could not come fast enough. They arrived at the dog track a little early. They didn't want to be late. They saw the sign on the door that said "Registration." They opened the door. Inside, there were already a few greyhounds and their trainers. When they entered the room everyone became very quiet. Mr. Prince was there, too, and so was Tazi. Mark recognized Mr. Prince and said, "Hello, Mr. Prince."

"What are your mutts doing in here? This room is just for Greyhounds," responded Mr. Prince.

Mark didn't expect Mr. Prince's response. "I thought you wanted to help Zora train for the dog races?" Mark inquired.

"Don't be silly. Your dog can't race with the Greyhounds. I only wanted to use your mongrel to help train Tazi. I never intended to help your mutt get into the races."

Mark, Zora, and Jackie stood silently for a moment. Dr. Rebecca Crumpler, the doctor that was there to give all the dogs their pre-race checkup, came over to see what was happening. She asked Mark why he had brought his dogs to the race track. He reached into his pocket and showed her the letter he had received from the Dog Racing Commission.

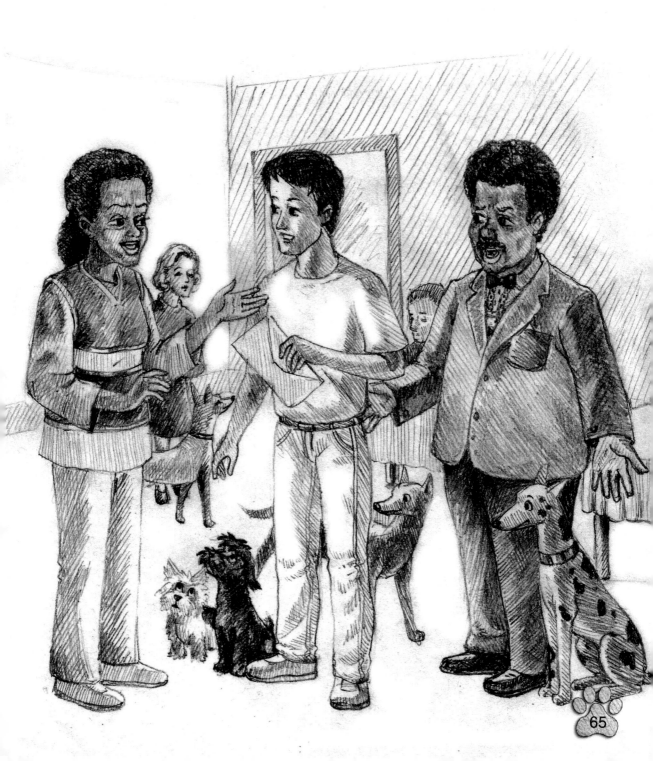

"This must be some kind of mistake, but the letter does say that Zora can race today," exclaimed Dr. Crumpler. "But we have never had any other breeds race except Greyhounds, so I don't know if we can let her race today," she went on to explain.

"The letter says that she can race," protested Mark.

"That mutt can't race!" hollered Mr. Prince.

Dr. Crumpler said calmly. "Why don't I weigh all the dogs and give them their pre-race exam. Then we will figure out which dogs are going to race. There are nine dogs entered today. Only eight will get to race."

Zora was worried. Maybe she wouldn't get to race after all.

They weighed her in first. She weighed in at 15 pounds and she passed her physical. Tazi weighed in next. He weighed 94 pounds. He was the biggest dog in the room.

"Son, my dog, Tazi, is going to run right over your puny little puppy," boasted Mr. Prince to Mark.

"All we want is a fair race," replied Mark. Zora barked in agreement. Even though she was little, she wasn't going to be afraid to run with the other dogs. She just wanted a chance to give it her doggone best.

ZORA AND THE GREYHOUNDS

Chapter 7

r. Crumpler completed all the dog exams. Now she had to assign all the dogs to their gates. There were eight gates, but nine dogs. Since Tazi was the reigning champ he was selected first. One by one the dogs were chosen for their gate position. There were two spots left. Dr. Crumpler called for Goliath—another one of the bigger Greyhounds.

Now there was only one spot left. Zora and Brett Lee were the two remaining dogs. Brett Lee had recorded one of the best times ever, but Dr. Crumpler had noticed he was limping around the locker room, so she took an X-ray of his paw. The X-ray showed that one of his paw bones was broken. He needed to rest his paw so that it could heal.

Dr. Crumpler couldn't let him run. There was only one dog left that could run. Zora was going to get the spot.

"Zora, it's your lucky day. Are you ready to race?" asked Dr. Crumpler.

Zora was sitting next to Jackie. When she heard the Doctor call her name she jumped up and ran over to give the Doctor a big lick.

Mark picked up Zora and gave her a big hug. "All your hard work has paid off. You made your dreams comes true!"

Zora wagged her tail. She ran to her gate where the judge slipped on her racing jacket and said, "Looks like you're lucky number 7! You look great Miss Zora."

Jackie was so proud of her friend for not giving up. She barked, "Good luck! I knew you could do it!"

Zora looked back at Jackie and barked, "Thanks!" Then she hustled up to the starting gate.

All the dogs took to their starting positions. The bell rang, Zora heard the squeak of the lure coming around the bend, and the gate lifted with a bang.

"And they're off!" shouted the announcer. Zora and the Greyhounds bolted out of their gates as the announcer called out their positions in the race.

"Go Zora Go! Go Zora Go!" Zora could hear her name being shouted by the crowd as she ran even faster.

She was finally running with the big dogs!

Join Zora next time for more adventures!

ABOUT THE AUTHOR

Mark A.J. Guilliatt lives in Omaha with his family and, of course, his real life dogs, Zora and Jackie.

When Mark isn't occupied by the assignments of his daily life, he is inspired by his worldwide travels and adventures to explore his myriad curiosities and daydreams.

Some of these daydreams may even reveal Zora's next big adventures, so please stay tuned to find out what Zora will be doing next.